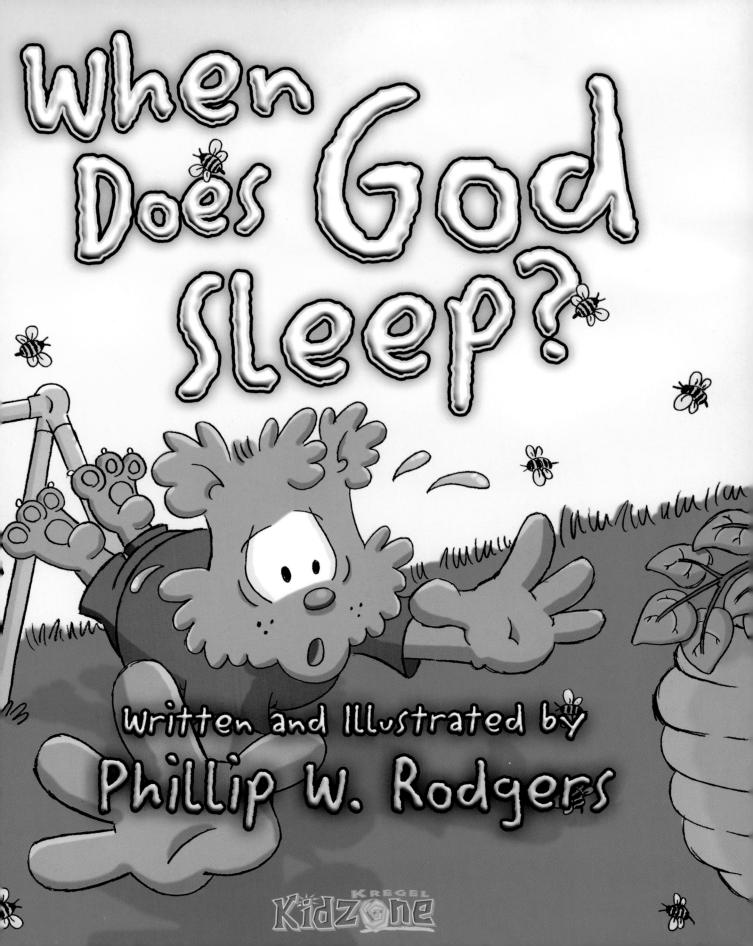

When Does God Sleep? © 2007 by Phillip W. Rodgers
Published by Kregel Kidzone, an imprint of Kregel Publications
Grand Rapids, Michigan 49501 USA.

A special thanks to Dennis Hillman and Stephen Barclift for their
dedication and editing expertise.

ISBN 13: 978-0-8254-3631-4

Printed in China

To
Stephanie,
Kaylee,
and Abby

One early fall morning
when the woodlands were cool,
young Bailey the Bear
was all ready for school.

His fur was twice-combed
from his toes to his chin,
but he sported a frown
instead of a grin.

"What's worrying my bear cub?"
his mom gently said
as she gave him a kiss
on the top of his head.

Bailey said, "I was wondering,
before I go,
if you knew when God sleeps?
I thought you might know."

"On a day like today, what
would happen instead
if God didn't get up, but just
stayed in His bed?"

"Why, God might miss something,"
young Bailey explained.
"I might slip off the slide,
and my paw could get sprained!"

"A fun day at school could turn bad in a minute
if God had a bed and was still sleeping in it."

"If I fell off a swing, I might skin my bear knees!
Or even fall into a nest of mad bees!"

"Or what if the slide was a mean alligator?
I'd need help right then, not wait until later."

"If God snores like Dad or He talks in His sleep,
I don't think He'll hear me. Not even a peep."

Bailey's mom was a wise bear
and always prepared
to say the right thing
to a cub who was scared.

"God's not like a bear cub
all snuggled in bed
with the covers pulled up
to the top of His head."

"God always takes care
of the world that He made.
He doesn't get tired
like a cub that has played."

"When you are in trouble,
God doesn't delay.
He'll comfort and calm you
whenever you pray."

It's OK.
I'm still here.
I love you.

"When God's people left Egypt,
He gave them a light
that sheltered and led them
by day and by night."

"Pharaoh sent out his army;
Moses sent up a plea,
and God saved them from Pharaoh
by parting the sea."

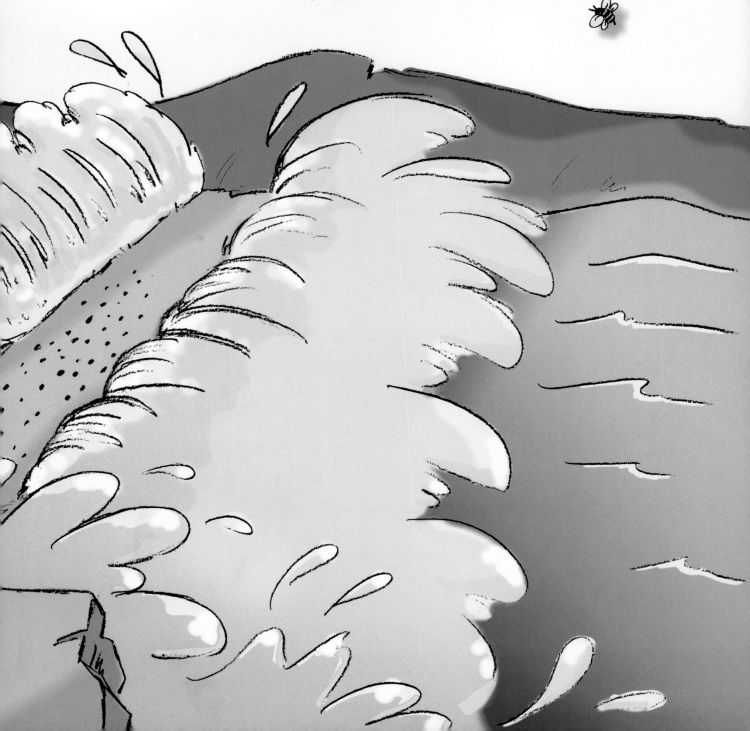

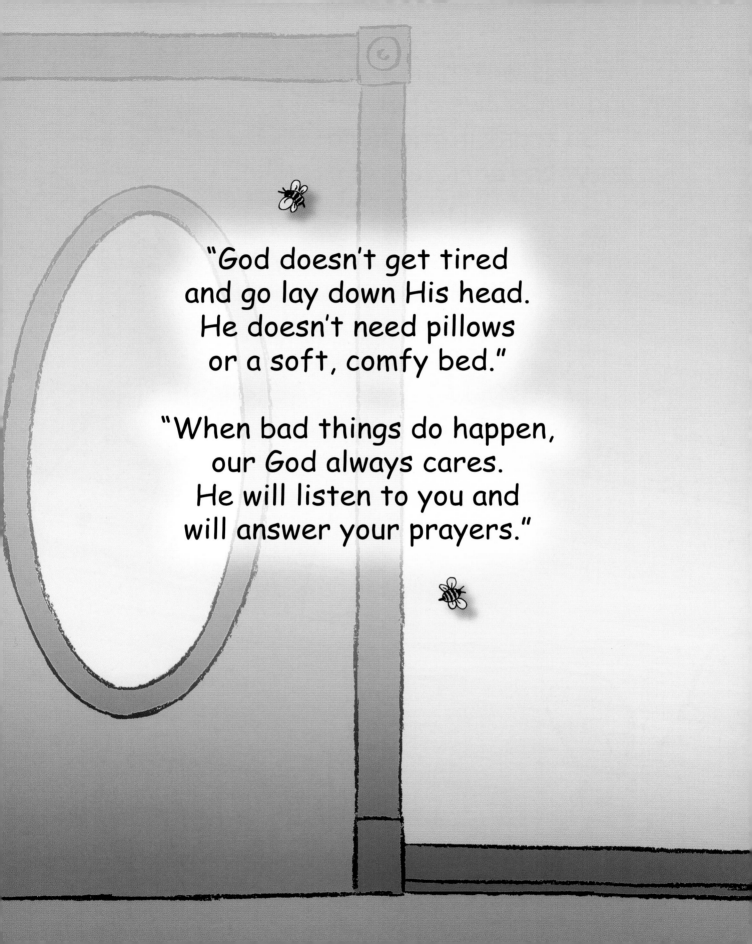

"God doesn't get tired
and go lay down His head.
He doesn't need pillows
or a soft, comfy bed."

"When bad things do happen,
our God always cares.
He will listen to you and
will answer your prayers."

"God is watching you, son,
and He knows what is best.
So trust in the Lord—
let your fears take a rest!"

"God really does see me!"
Bailey said with delight.
"He'll watch me all day
and be with me all night!"

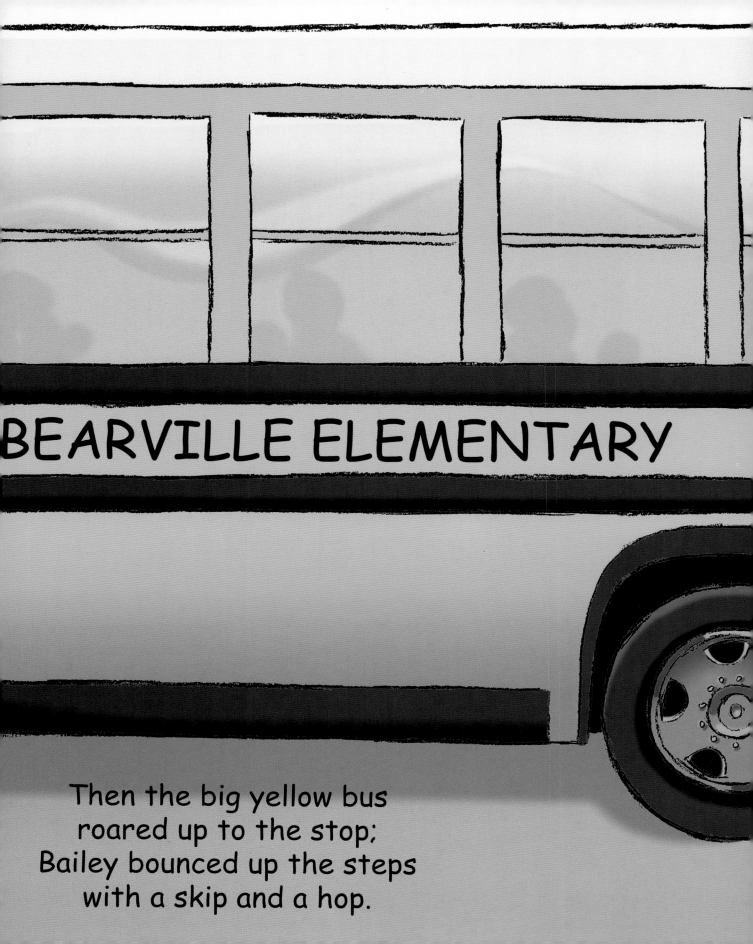

Then the big yellow bus
roared up to the stop;
Bailey bounced up the steps
with a skip and a hop.

Bailey walked down the aisle
and sat in the rear.
Then he prayed, "Thank You, God.
I know You are near!"

He waved to his mom as the bus pulled away,
and he knew it would be a really great day.